Apres Le Deluge – The Drought is Over

Introduction

When I started what I will describe as an epic journey, I never thought that it would end up with six books of verse, and a novel.

I started writing at the beginning of the Covid 19 lockdown in Wales in March 2020. I had begun watching the Outlander series at around the same time.

Since my retirement as a Police Officer in 2013, I have been volunteering several times a week with the two groups of Riding for the Disabled which operate in my local area. During lockdown it was necessary for them to cease operation.

Our Patron Princess Anne the Princess Royal made an appeal for fund raising.

I began by publishing a book of Horse and Covid Lockdown related poems any revenue generated to be donated to RDA.

Then I posted a very tongue in cheek poem on the Outlander Series Books and TV site. A number of readers asked if I had written anymore similar works.

After I had written and posted a few more – readers asked whether I had published them.

So here I am with due deference to Diana Gabaldon six books later.

In the meantime, Season Six has been filmed and wrapped. Diana has given a publishing date for book 9 'Go Tell the Bees that I am Gone'.

The Drought is over, and the rain has come, we are now 'Après Le Deluge'.

This is a book written by a fan of the Outlander Books and the TV series, for fans – it is not an Official Outlander Publication, though I do publish with the goodwill of Diana's agents.

I try not to deviate from the original plot lines and to put a poetic twist on the story and sometimes see a situation from another viewpoint.

The cover is rather special front cover is a pastel artwork produced by a fellow fan and used with her permission. Thank You Lyn Fuller

Readers, you seem to have enjoyed my last efforts, I hope you will enjoy this one.

Contents

Introduction 2

Outlander Day 2021 7

A small draught horse 8

Oats for Breakfast! 10

A game of chess 12

Memorial Day 14

Orthopaedics and Alcohol 15

A lesson in Ghailig 17

Adewayhe 19

Made from memory! 21

Missing in Action 23

Squeaky Noises 26

Sword play 28

The Void 30

Unfinished business 32

Understanding Women 34

Understanding Men 37

Glass Face 39

Tragedy 41

Quad Erat Demonstrandum 45

A letter to America 47

Attention Soldier!.. 49

Invasion.. 51

Deserters.. 53

Horrocks... 56

Master Raymond 58

Penance 59

Soldier On 61

Take me home 63

Wiley Mr Wylie 65

Held Hostage 67

Lust... 70

Plotting Murder 72

St Germaine 74

The Other Woman... 75

Time and motion 77

Debt of Honour.. 80

And one more thing! 82

Death's door 84

Kissing the wilderness 86

Aldwych Farce. 88

Always Forever 90

Unrest – Tar and feather bed 92

The Fiddler on the Roof.. 94

Seeing Red 96

Grand Da has Balls.. 98

Calls in the Forest 100

Telephone for Grand Da 102

L.O.V.E... 104

Outlander Animals 105

Things you win at dice! 106

Wolf Brothers 108

Bacon on the run. 110

'Beware of the Pig!!... 112

A verra noisy mule... 114

Adso – a cat with attitude 116

Major MacDonald's Wig.. 118

Donas – sire of generations 120

Gideon 122

Acknowledgements... 124

Other books by the Author 125

Copyright.. 126

Outlander Day 2021

The books are read, the series viewed,
From different points of view,
Fans from round the world discuss,
That's just what we do.

There are crafters, there are artists,
All talented you know,
Raising money making things,
Inspired by the show!

Money raised for charities,
And keeping ourselves sane,
Especially in these strange times,
If we get locked down again.

Debates are held in private,
We support the cast and crew,
Now get on with season six,
The Fandom waits for you!

**

A small draught horse

Where did this woman come from?
She is nae like the rest,
She speaks her mind, she's feisty,
And she's sitting on my chest!

She's already fixed ma shoulder,
She knows just what she's doin!
If it was left to Angus,
My arm would be a ruin.

All the way to Leoch,
She's sat between my thighs,
The feelings rather pleasant,
Ken, she doesn't realise!

It's nice and warm wrapped in his plaid,
I feel his body heat,
I won't admit to feeling more,
That would be indiscreet.

But he's very damned attractive,
I could sit like this all day.
Hell, I'm a married woman!
I shouldn't feel this way!

I'll tend his wounds,
My god his back! He's open with his past,
He frankly tells me everything,
From the first stroke to the last.

Who is this boy, who comforts me?
He's got my senses wired,
I feel that underneath his kilt,
He's really not that tired!

**

Oats for Breakfast!

What a way to start the day,
Only half awake,
A warrior's hands upon my thighs,
I like this – no mistake,

Soft lips have wandered down my skin,
Exploring every nook,
Tongue and teeth are all in play,
I know that blue eyed look,

He lost himself in pleasure,
There's banging on the door,
Don't stop now, ignore it,
Use that tongue some more.

Wake up! We can't be more awake,
Intent on giving pleasure,
After this I'll pay him back
At least in equal measure.

No! He will not be put off,
He's finishing the job,
Murtagh banging on the door,
Will not this pleasure rob.

Are ye worn out Jamie,
From servicing yer wife,
That ye can'nae rise from bed,
Not to save your life.

I groan a bit in pleasure,
And hide beneath the sheet,
Murtagh looks embarrassed,
He has been indiscreet!

**

A game of chess

King's pawn two, the opening move
Bishops pawn reply.
A game of skill and tactics,
They sit there, eye to eye,

The prisoner and the Governor,
A most unlikely game,
A friendship of necessity,
Of need and mutual gain.

Knight's pawn two, Queen to fools mate.
The port is poured tonight.
The gambit turns to Frenchman's gold,
Sent to the Jacobite.

Discussion moves to dangerous ground,
Of loves and families lost,
The cut and thrust of mental games,
Who will give the most!

He reaches out, a hand is touched,
It moves, he lets his lie,
A look to turn a man to stone,
A battle- hardened eye.

You cannot know just what you do,
How your touch will end,
Remove your hand or you will die,
I am not that form of friend.

He rises graceful from the chair,
Your contact burns his skin,
Touch him and he'll kill you,
He will never let you in.

✳✳

Memorial Day

Battles lost, battles won,
The long fight to be free,
From government remote and far
removed across the sea.

An Immigration nation,
Home to those that fled,
Sent in chains or taken, slaves,
A Sentence to be dead.

Governed by oppressors.
There is a better way,
Those that fought the fight and won,
Are the USA today.

**

Orthopaedics and Alcohol

Rolled up in a dirty plaid,
More dead than alive,
A pulse so faint and thready,
I pray he will survive.

Laid out on MacCrannoch's hearth,
Bleeding on the rug,
I offer him the laudanum,
He won't accept the drug,

Surgery on his fractured hand
Will mean a wealth of pain,
If it's left to heal alone
He won't use it again.

Gaelic cursing, muffled prayer,
A gag between his teeth,
He bids me do what I must do,
With whisky pain relief.

Bones pushed back beneath the skin,
Splints to hold them fast.
Stitches in to close the wounds.
I'm nearly done at last!

Clean the lot with alcohol,
He's sweating now with strain,
Begging me to shoot him,
And vomiting with pain!

Sir Marcus was a soldier,
Unflappable for sure,
He urges me complete my work,
He's heard men scream before!

Drunk with whisky, Wounds now dressed,
On Annabelle's best rugs
The patient falls to fitful rest,
Without the use of drugs,

I cannot sleep, I sit with him,
Quiet and alone,
And listen to his breathing,
With a large dram of my own.

**

A lesson in Ghailig

Jem was bunking off from school,
Running up the hill,
Heading for his grand da's cave,
He had time to kill.

Dodging worn out rutting stags,
I followed his red hair,
I found him at the cask leap,
Hiding in his lair.

He said he was nae fighting,
He had nae thrown a fist,
Just used a bit of Ghailig,
To a boy who got the gist!

Teased for being Papist,
And told he'd burn in hell,
Jem's riposte was sure and swift,
He'd see him there as well!

Enter Miss Glendenning,
She'd pulled him by his ear,
Punished him for nothing,
Jem's sense of fairness here!

Then he'd lost his temper,
And in not too many phases,
Cursed her up in Ghailig,
Using Grand da's, best bad phrases!

Miss Glendenning did nae understand,
A word of what was said,
Mr Menzies on the other hand,
Is fluent! – Jem was dead!

So young Jem got his arse strapped,
And ran away from school,
Then hid up on the mountain,
Feeling like a fool.

A Jamie Fraser cursing,
In barbaric Erse,
Is a wondrous thing to hear,
No sentiment is worse.

He's so much like, his Grand Da,
I'm sure they have connection,
I can hear it now across the void,
Every damned inflection.

**

Adewayhe

Her face
Is worn by life and time,
weathered by the years,
A mantle worn with quiet pride,
With the wisdom of the Seers.

Her Eyes
Deep pools of darkness,
A stillness filled with light,
All seeing, and all knowing,
Through time she has the sight.

Her smile
A peaceful blessing,
A calmness sure and true,
She reads the soul before her,
She knows the strength in you.

She speaks,
Her quiet wisdom,
Her words may leave you numb,
She tells you to absolve you,
She sees now, what will come,

Her End
Death is not your fault my friend,
We cannot fight the odds,
You must not always blame yourself,
Death comes from the Gods.

Murdered.
Killed by one whose ignorance,
Would not let him forgive,
Whose eyes only saw savages,
Who would not let him live.

The Gift
Her hair was whiter than the snow,
The blood still stained the cloth,
His vengeance on the pure of soul
Had vented out his wrath.

The Fire
You sent her out with reverence,
Released now to the wind,
Her people will avenge her soul,
Fire will be the end.

**

Made from memory!

A blade must know it's owner,
Then it will nae do you harm,
I rummaged in my pocket,
Half a shilling crossed his palm,

It glinted in the setting sun,
Sharp to cut the night,
A knife must have a job to do,
And you must teach it right,

He ran its edge across his thumb,
The red began to well,
Now it knows the taste of blood,
Its purpose it can tell.

No romantic gesture this,
Tis a gift that I will need,
To keep me safe, when in harm's way.
A thoughtful gift indeed.

I prick my thumb, it joins with his,
He is my blood and bone,
Repeat the oath I took that day,
To live our lives as one.

The handle smoothed from antler,
Fits perfect in my hand,
Contoured all from memory?
I don't quite understand!

How is it carved exactly?
The reply, a gentle mock!
Eyebrow raised, with half a smile,
Your hand around my cock!

**

Missing in Action

Fighting ceased,
The silence, broken by the cries,
The moaning of the wounded,
Each in his own blood lies.

The scavengers and looters,
Robbing from the dead,
Stealing from the wounded,
Anything for bread!

Familiar in shape and form,
Lying in the dirt,
Long legs splayed, not moving!
Face down and inert!

A boy searching his pockets,
Then takes out a knife,
'I'll cut his throat, shall I mam?
He's ours then for life.

The sword is heavy in my hands,
I pull it from the mud,
Two handed swing it round my head,
A lethal rush of blood.

They will not have him either way,
In life and death, he's mine,
Even if he's missing bits,
That will suit me fine.

Alive, and I'm berating him,
relief and anger too
Yelling like a fishwife,
The language of a shrew,

Vainglorious Scottish bastard,
You must tell me now, of course,
How you fought off that dragoon
By screaming at his horse

Your hand is chopped to dog-meat,
Your face is bruised to hell,
Are you going to tell me next?
You fought the horse as well!

He had to play the hero,
Break the bloody charge,
Balls the size of ten- pound shot!
I don't think they're that large!

Strapped up and exhausted,
I lay him down to rest,
Underneath the waggon,
Hand strapped across his chest.

Before we left the battlefield
He thanked me for his life,
Praised my wielding of his sword,
Not common in a wife.

Later I'll repair him,
For now, I'll let him linger,
On just what pain he will go through,
When I amputate that finger!

**

Squeaky Noises

Why is it that they scratch their balls?
It's just because they can!
Naked in their universe,
Just being a man.

Curious shades of body hair,
Add a touch of spice,
And when you've been three months at sea,
Don't forget the lice!

Beards can be such sensual things,
Erotic to the touch,
Don't make plans to shave just yet,
I've planned for this so much,

Not half of what I've planned for you,
Ye maker of wee sounds,
When I get you on the shore, alone.
I shall make ye howl like hounds!

Hot water and some vinegar,
You're having a good scrub,
Keep your infestation,
Confined to the tub.

I'll have ye lie a top o me,
Yer arse I love tae squeeze,
I've not had room tae do these things,
Since we've been on the seas,

A soapy kiss, a testing grope,
His touch is all allure,
He's smelling more like Jamie now,
Much less like a sewer,

Now, captain of the Artemis,
Before we put to sea,
Plans, reclamation of his wife,
The sound effects come free!

Louse free, scrubbed, and shiny,
Anticipating pleasure,
Shall I take him somewhere very quiet,
And scratch his balls at leisure!

**

Sword play

The blade is tailored to his arm,
The balance is perfection,
Limb and sword in harmony,
His body's sharp extension.

A graceful form of deadly art,
Strength and skill are pleated,
Woven into metal spells,
A magic undefeated.

Flowing moves as smooth as silk,
Focused, no distraction,
A subtle dance on cat like feet,
A body primed for action.

I watch him practice, mesmerised,
First left hand and then right,
Two handed with the Claymore,
His mind is in the fight.

He promised me protection,
Of his family and name,
And lastly with the body,
So proficient at this game

Feline in his actions,
A master of this art,
A warrior trained from childhood,
I cannot break his heart.

＊＊

The Void

How often, will we take a breath,
And stare into the void
Look with dread over the edge,
Our sense of worth destroyed,

The point of your existence,
The reason for your life,
Your fear of death, of nothingness,
Will cut you like a knife.

How life is treated cheaply,
Wasted, thrown away,
Does no one have a duty?
To try at least to stay.

I know that he has seen the void,
More frequently than I,
A warrior's end, is purposeful,
He is not afraid to die.

Tears are running down my face,
I cry without a cause.
Are my efforts pointless,
Healing at deaths door.

Is the night sky not a void?
He tries to draw me out,
Look up and you see the stars,
They will not go out.

Nothing is ever lost ye see,
Mankind will always hope,
we two will exist just the same,
With all of this we'll cope.

We hear the sound of music,
The chiming of a bell,
I must check on my patient.
Nine O'clock and all is well.

Life will go on around us,
We will not give up the fight,
Don't look down at the darkness,
Look up, to the light.

**

unfinished business

Balriggan, is a lovely spot,
A calm and tranquil place,
Why did I choose to go there?
Just to show my face,

Maybe curiosity,
I knew she had a man,
Maybe to apologise,
Was that part of my plan?

Mistakes I made when I was young,
I should have told her then,
I never was in love with her,
Men played with her ye ken.

I never would have married her,
She was too young and bold as brass,
She'd never live the life I'd lead,
She'll always be a lass!

Jenny wanted happiness,
With me right by her side,
The only way she'd have it,
Was if I took a bride.

I tried my best to please them all,
With the part of me war left,
Most of me was far away,
Desolate, bereft.

She has nae changed her attitude,
She will not even listen,
Still blames me for all her ills,
If she had a brain, it's missin'!

She will nae marry Joey,
She'd rather live, in sin.
Then I have to keep her,
And she's money coming in.

I've said that I am sorry,
I can'nae say much more,
Then I'm dodging flower- pots
And fighting on the floor,

I'll let the water, of the Loch.
Calm me of this care,
I've washed Laoghaire Mackenzie.
Right out of my hair.

**

Understanding Women

In all the times I've lain with him,
He's never touched me so,
As if he's bored, no feeling there,
Monotonous and slow.

Harsh, and with no feeling,
Going through the motions,
The penny drops, I know his mind,
Is far across an ocean.

My angry scream brings him awake,
Consciousness has dawned,
Confusion, drives him from our bed,
Frustration, I am warned!

Why ......? He does not love her,
Is he jealous of another?
Why......? He does not want her,
he knows she has a lover.

He doubts his male ability,
He tried every wile invented,
Was it him or was it her?
His pride is sorely dented.

Logic does not play a part,
His mind is slowly sinking.
Another man fulfils her,
His inner Caveman, thinking!

The fact he can't abide her,
Really doesn't matter,
His prowess between the sheets,
Male ego, he must flatter,

If he could read the female mind,
Then he would plainly see,
The problem was in Laoghaire's mind,
She knew he was with me!

Do I ever think of Frank?
The question hangs above.
Frank is dead, he is a ghost,
I do not choose to love!

Maybe we should leave our ghosts,
They may just find each other,
Laoghaire with the ghost of Frank
Now there's a thought my lover.

Stop beating on your caveman chest,
Stop taking all the blame,
Women are a fickle breed,
We are not all the same.

And if you love THIS woman,
There's no more to be said!
It's bloody cold, I'm freezing!
Take me back to bed!

✳✳

Understanding Men

Both had been imprisoned,
Both honourable men,
Neither one will give an inch.
Like rams fenced in a pen,

Butting heads, a contest,
Which one is the stronger,
I'd bet Mr Fraser,
Will last out the longer,

I'd sewn up Tom Christie's hand,
With no pain relief,
With Jamie there he would not flinch
He'd groan through gritted teeth,

They play a game of cat and mouse,
Verbal barbs, and taunts,
One, mentions honour in his scars,
One Bible knowledge flaunts.

Each testing the other,
They fight with verbal swords,
Who will Lose their cool, to temper?
In this game of words,

Christie has the last word,
Going through the door,
But Jamie's laughing – eyebrow raised,
He's seen it all before.

Opposite in many ways,
But really just the same,
Men like Christie needed,
If we are to win the game.

I don't think I can understand,
Why they never stop,
The constant competition,
The need to be on top.

Sassenach don't fool yourself,
You ken men all too well,
You'd like to think you din nae,
For it is the road to hell.

Tom Christie is a fighter,
When is nose is out of joint,
He'll fight hard to keep his place,
And that is just the point.

Glass Face

My countenance transparent,
I have a face of glass,
There is no blind, or filter,
To hide the thoughts that pass.

That man there at the trading post,
I thought I had forgot,
When that night came flooding back,
I knew that I had not.

I do not do pretence that well!
A signal plainly writ,
I'm fretful about something,
And he'll find the cause of it.

Maybe not directly,
I may not want to tell,
But he has his wily ways,
And a crock of it he smells!

I try prevarication,
tell him half a tale,
Knowing that it will not wash,
His instincts do not fail.

I know there will be fall out,
A truth I cannot give.,
Kill them all – was what he meant.
He will not let him live!

Consuming passion under stars,
Then gone in the night,
He'd find out what he needed,
My problem now his fight.

Three days gone, he's home at last,
Cheerful, bearing deer,
A most successful hunting trip,
At least that's what I fear.

We give our hearts to many,
Always free to roam,
Our own are in each, other's hands.
For we are each, others home.

**

Tragedy

Smoke!
I dreamed of Cigarettes and Frank,
Our loft was filled with smoke,
Fire! I screamed in terror,
My sleeping man awoke!

Flames!
Get out now, he yelled at me,
Don't bother to dress,
Wake the others quickly,
Get them from this mess.

Panic!
Falling down the ladder,
Landing in a heap,
Shouting, raising the alarm!
Waking all from sleep.

Fire!
Fire is in the print shop,
Stacks of bibles burn,
Get the weans out Marsali!
Or we'll all cook to a turn.

Woken!
Felicite and Joanie
Stir their sleepy heads,
Where are Henri and Germaine?
They haven't used their beds.

Lost!
Standing half dressed in the street,
Watching our lives burn,
Where the hell are those two boys
Will they never learn.

Trapped!
Emerging on the rooftop,
Trapped there by the flames.
Sleeping in the starlight,
Not the best of games.

Danger!
Throw your little brother!
But Henri would not go,
Terrified he looked at us,
In the street below.

No!
Germaine! he is too heavy,
He cannot hold on,
His little arms and shortened legs,
He really isn't strong.

Falling!
He slipped so slowly from his grip,
Somersaulted down,
Fell through all the waiting arms,
Landing on his crown.

Dead!
The sickening thud upon the ground,
The screaming of his mother,
The family had lost a son.
Germaine, his little brother.

Arson!
How was the fire started?
Was it set, to start?
Fergus never left the forge,
Alight when it was dark.

Rebuilding!
All we have is Clarence,
And what's rescued from the blaze.
The clothes that we stand up in.
At least it burned my stays!

Loss!
A family in mourning,
Focussed, in our thought,
The loss of Henri- Christian,
And all the joy he brought.

Leaving!
We will leave Philadelphia,
Jamie, take me now!
Back to our home Frasers Ridge,
We will find a way somehow!

**

Quad Erat Demonstrandum

Necessity the old wives say,
Is mother of invention,
How adept we have become
At hiding our intention.

All our wealth is melted down,
Mundane things are made,
Rifle shot made out of gold,
Tools, of the soldier's trade.

Two sets of typeset letters,
Rolled in dirt and grease,
We would not need, to do these things,
If these were times of peace.

All lost in that fire,
Which someone set by stealth
A child lost, a soul that's mourned,
Is worth far more than wealth,

Counting up our losses,
We formulate a plan,
To get us all to safety,
Savannah if we can.

Found amongst the ruins,
A grimy bag of lead,
What use now without a press.
The printing business dead.

Caslon English Roman,
For printing things in Latin,
The font for Papist prayer books,
Which bag shall we pack that in?

He smiles and tips the letters out,
He scratches off the dirt,
A gleam of gold beneath the grime,
His face becomes alert.

Fortunes change in instants,
Poverty removed.
Quad Erat Demonstrandum
Our plan is now approved.

Q.E.D

**

A letter to America

The writer writes with Quill, and ink,
On parchment stiff and old,
A friend is gone, his end is come,
His body has grown cold.

A stilted hand, aches with time,
It crawls across the page,
Tears, flow, the ink will run,
With sadness, not with rage.

He writes across the endless sea,
He writes to his love, who waits,
He writes to ease the endless ache,
The loss of Ian creates.

He writes of telling stories,
Told to pass the time,
A raconteur of talent,
Discoursing in his prime,

He worries for his sister,
Her grief is inward turned,
Living now within her shell
Her outer layers burned.

He tells her they will start for home,
They leave the shores of France,
Passage booked on the Euterpe,
And so, begins a dance!

He yearns to lie beside her,
To feel her touch, anon
Sorrow writes the final page,
The ink- stained wretch signs off!

**

Attention Soldier!

Lay your head now Soldier,
Let me ease your mind,
Rest it here upon my breast,
Some comfort you may find,

Shoulders back now Soldier,
Let me apply the oil,
Set free the trials of the day,
Distract you from your toil,

About turn! Soldier,
I run my palms all down your back,
Tracing out those ancient scars,
Hands iron out each crack.

Now rest easy Soldier,
You are safe under my hands,
Muscles torn from acts of war,
Stretch like elastic bands.

(What is one of those Sassenach?)

Is it time for action Soldier?
The parts I have not mentioned,
Have listened to my Sergeants drill,
Look you're standing to attention!

Quit yer talking Sassenach,
Come and make some squeaks!
You know, the ones I like the most,
I've not heard them for weeks,

Shall I pin ye underneath me,
When ye've oiled me some more,
Then you'll make some noises
That you've never made before!

**

Invasion

Jamie climbed into our bed,
Just before the dawn
He smelled of marsh and fish and frogs,
And just a bit of prawn.

Good fishing then? Aye, not too bad
He told me what they saw,
Soldiers marching, troop on troop,
Warships off the shore!

The British Army landing,
A dozen men- o-war,
Here comes the revolution!
Knocking on our door.

At supper time we had a knock
The Continentals calling,
You are needed General Fraser Sir,
Their manner was appalling.

They cannot see discretion,
That their cause is lost,
Live to fight another day,
Or you will count the cost,

He will not fight, not this time,
For this is not his battle,
He sees the Continentals,
Will be rounded up like cattle.

Now accused of cowardice
The Scot is losing patience,
Dia eadarainn's an t-olc,"
Is lost in the translation.

Go with God but leave my house!
I will nae shake yer hand.
My commission is resigned,
I've told ye where I stand.

Prepare for occupation,
Not quite what we planned,
We must live with the British,
I shall keep my knife at hand.

✷✷

Deserters

The feel of being marrit,
Was new upon my bones,
I could na really speak with her,
Save when we're alone,

Travelling in company,
Teasing from the men,
She'll give them back a lot of it,
She's a fine quick wit ye ken,

They've taught her how to use a knife,
She's verra quick tae learn,
But could she really kill a man,
I'll find out in my turn.

We ventured up the hillside,
To fill the skins with water,
Feeling kind of amorous,
More often than we oughta!

The feel of sun upon my back,
And woman's flesh below,
She makes me feel like God on earth,
Her touch sets me a glow,

Loving in the long grass,
Joking having fun,
I hear a click behind my head,
the barrel of a gun.

Deserters from the army,
Desperate, on the run,
Would rape my wife before my eyes,
Before the morn was done.

I watch her close, my temper held!
I see signals in her eyes,
As she tempts that Red Coat bastard,
By opening her thighs!

I had to hold my feelings,
Let my anger burn,
As Claire enticed the Redcoat
To the point of no return.

Filthy bastard that he is,
His gun against my head,
My captor eggs his comrade on,
He may well end up dead.

She grabs his neck and pulls him down,
A false sense of embrace,
A knife is drawn out from her skirt,
She stabs! and hits the place,

A spurt of blood, the jerk of pain,
The second blow will tell,
Straight up to his kidneys,
Wee Angus taught ye well!

My hand is swift, upon my dirk,
My captors throat is cut,
A pistol shot, into the air,
Too late to save the scut,

Crawling from beneath that man,
Bloody hands and knife,
Shaking, trembling, warrior brave,
She has just saved my life.

Be careful on the mountainside,
When yer wife ye bed,
Ye may just get a Redcoat,
Put a pistol to yer head!

**

Horrocks

Horrocks, had the blarney!
He talked with Irish charm.
So badly did I want reprieve,
I did not hear the alarm.

Why would the Kings deserter?
Want to help my cause,
Gold his motivation,
Blackmail his recourse.

'I told ye I'd give ye a name,
A name is what ye've got,
The fact it is no use to ye,
Concerns me not one jot.'

I saw it all I told ye,
I cannot tell ye why,
Best you ask Jack Randall,
Why his Sergeant had to die.

I'll take the gold, it please ye,
Sure, I've told ye true,
I met ye and I spoke with ye,
I don't care what you do.

So, Horrocks did me over,
Deception is his game,
I'll have to find some other way,
To finally to clear my name!

**

Master Raymond

The oldest of the ancients,
A soul older than time,
Blue Aura of a healer,
Sorcerer sublime.

Purveyor of antiquities,
The pickled and the rare,
His little shop in Paris,
You'll find it all in there.

Caecilian in appearance,
A twinkle in his eye,
He walks a fine line around the law,
The King would have him die.

He has seen a thousand years,
Been born a hundred times,
Dabbles in the darker arts,
Capital his crimes.

Vanishing from Paris,
Unsafe to remain,
Master of the holes in time,
Will we see you back again?

**

Penance

He sold you into wedlock,
His spoiled and headstrong child,
Arrogant impetuous,
And just a wee bit wild.

You would' na' do it quietly,
You could nae just get wed,
To a man old as yer grand sire,
Because of that you're dead,

You wanted one experience,
To set your body free,
You got just what you wanted,
You are dead because of me!

If I had nae done it,
If I had told you no,
There would have been no baby,
To rip yer insides so!

So, I will watch your coffin,
In penance on the floor,
Brave girl, I did' nae love you,
I told you that before.

I was blind with aching need,
I used you for release,
You died, and I will blame myself,
My guilt will never cease.

The child I will not raise is mine,
You have given me a son,
For that I always thank you,
But my penance must be done.

Endless awkward questions,
I will not be drawn,
My prayer for redemption done.
Grey will watch you til the dawn.

**

Soldier On

I'd told him all, the words had flowed,
From me like a spout,
Like water running in a burn,
The truth was finally out.

He took me back, right to the stones,
Time now for revision,
Back to Frank or stay with him!
Finality, Decision.

Back to explanation,
Back to modern things,
Back to a life more complex,
Safety's what it brings.

Stay with death and danger,
Stay with want and war,
Stay and face a thousand things.
You've never faced before.

Step back through the stones again,
And this will be all gone,
Consign it all to history,
Forget you were as one.

I ask the stones for guidance,
Decision made! I'm done.
I must get to the Cot house,
Before the set of sun.

I would not miss convenience,
But I would miss his laugh,
I would miss his hands on me,
Hmm I would miss a nice hot bath.

I cannot walk away from him,
He needs me, as his breath,
He makes me whole as I do him,
I'm bound to him till death.

Frank will make another life,
He'll move on and he'll thrive,
I know he will get over me.
I know he will survive.

He lies there by the fire,
Crying in his sleep,
Tears running down his cheek,
His watch for me he keeps.

I could not do it soldier,
I could not break the bond.
An oath in blood will bind me,
I will gladly soldier on

Take me home

Home is not just where you live,
It's where your heart is whole,
A place where all your bits are one,
Body, mind, and soul.

Home is in your happy place,
It could be anywhere,
It needs no bricks and mortar,
It needs no room to spare.

When I am on a hillside,
Staring at the sea,
Watching waves break on the rocks,
This could be home for me.

Sometimes I don't need people,
To clutter up the place,
I just need time to clear my mind,
I just need empty space.

So, when your feet get itchy,
And you feel it's time to roam,
Remember the coordinates,
Of what you call your home.

For when your roaming's finished,
On your feet, or in your mind,
Home is there with open arms,
Come in, and rest you'll find.

**

Wiley Mr Wylie

Arrogant, and foppish,
His make- up and his wig,
His over courteous manners,
Lipstick on a pig!

He thinks himself a man of style,
With words that paint him pretty,
He flatters, and insinuates,
But isn't very witty.

Women are a conquest,
A notch upon his sword,
To turn him down, unheard of.
God's gift thinks he is adored.

A dandy in his satins,
All fashion in his silks,
Walking cane, beauty spot,
The crowd he always milks.

In league with the devil,
That's how he funds his life,
And sets his cap for an affair,
With Jamie Frasers wife.

Persistent in advances,
Abhorrent to his core,
Claire may be in trouble,
He will force his case for sure.

Her ever watchful husband,
Looking for his wife,
He knows just where to find her,
For she is his life.

There really is no contest,
In what will come to pass,
An angry Jamie Fraser
Will sit Wylie on his arse.

A short interrogation,
On threat of certain pain
A deal is done, for Bonnet's life,
And Claire can breathe again.

**

Held Hostage

I'm searching for my brother John,
He's missing, who knows where,
My blood is up, I'm fuming!
Is he kidnapped? But who'd dare!

My chest feels tight I cannot breathe,
My remedy not working.
If I collapse out in the street,
I'll be robbed for certain.

Who is this bloody woman?
She's taken all my clothes,
She's feeding me the strangest tea,
And smoke blown up my nose!

And I am in my brother's house,
At least that's what she said,
But even though I'm breathing,
She won't let me out of bed.

What's this, they're writing letters,
Pretending to be John.
I think I'm being kept here,
for a reason. Hell, Anon.

This woman is my brother's wife,
How could this come to be!
Women do not serve his needs,
His queer proclivities!

Good God I've been here ages,
Sitting in my shirt,
I can hear the drums approaching,
The rebel army dirt!

These women have some brass neck,
They're lying to the army,
Kidnapping Lord Melton
They really both are barmy.

Lord Melton! Jenny points the gun,
Twas you that killed my man,
Locked him in a prison,
Where his lingering death began!

Softly footed as a cat,
He walked into the room,
To see his sister blazing mad,
And the Lord to meet his doom.

Without a sound, the pistol grabbed!
The point -blank shot diverted,
His sister Jenny thus disarmed,
A crisis is averted.

Your servant Mr Fraser Sir,
Most obedient – your grace,
I see ye've met my sister,
By the look upon yer face!

**

Lust

He sat out in the prison yard,
His noble features proud,
Eyes burning, ever watchful,
Attentive in the crowd,

All hearing and all seeing,
noting my arrival,
A change of Governor will impact,
On prisoner survival.

The only man the jailers fear,
The only man in chains,
He is the very devil!
Colonel Quarry now explains.

He is a man of learning,
The man commands respect,
He speaks for the prisoners,
Their spokesman, elect.

The name Red Jamie Fraser,
Ripples down my spine,
He and I have history,
He should be no friend of mine.

He shrugs down in his blanket,
Talks softly to his men,
Walks quietly back into the cell,
The fox gone to his den.

In time I grow to like him,
He is erudite, urbane,
Like me he lost someone he loves,
I can feel his pain.

I'll not send him over oceans,
I shall keep him close by me,
Something deep inside my heart,
Won't let me set him free.

My mind covets his body,
That part I can't possess,
I will settle for his friendship,
a thing words cannot express.

**

Plotting Murder

Empty stables told the tale,
But one horse was kept,
Old Alec slept amongst the hay,
With his one eye he wept,

Starving men, no food to eat,
A need to feed the forces,
This last stand had all been planned,
Butcher all the horses,

The Bonnie Prince was in command,
He listened to God only,
By Gods right he'd win the day,
A leader's role is lonely,

But one way to stop the fate,
One way to save the Scots,
We're talking of a murder,
The most devious of plots,

No good comes of listening,
Hid behind a door,
To plan the death of Dougal's Prince,
He heard it all for sure,

Seducer and enchantress!
He called me whore, and bitch!
I'd grabbed his nephew with my claws,
I'm a traitor and a witch,

His dirk was drawn, he'd slit my throat,
His rage intent on death,
To poison his beloved Prince,
I'd draw no more breath,

Blood lust was upon him,
His nephew too must die,
His face was drawn in half- starved rage,
Madness in his eyes,

Uncle fought with nephew!
Tangled on the floor,
One dirk held between them,
The outcome so unsure.

I didn't hear the words he gasped,
When it pierced his throat,
It was either him or Jamie,
Would keep the Clan afloat,

Robbed of hearing music,
All those years ago,
Twas Dougal s axe that broke his head,
The bastard just said so.

St Germaine

Of the French nobility,
A dashing looking man,
Dressed in Paris fashion,
Meet Count St Germaine,

Ruthless in his dealings,
All manners and good grace,
Mysterious and secretive,
Despite that handsome face,

Magic Blacker than the night,
He seeks only to harm,
To further his own interests,
He'll use his evil charm.

Eels are not so slippery,
His life regenerates,
By moving through the veil of time,
Before he meets his fate.

How stealthily he dodges death,
He will return we know,
Nothing good will come of it,
The Comte is Black of soul.

The Other Woman

My master loves me dearly,
Looks after me with care,
Keeps me in the prime of life,
Makes sure my parts don't wear!

A beauty, made of iron,
Crafted to impress,
Smooth of operation,
My workings he'll caress.

I am well versed in Latin,
Hymn sheets and the Bible
Treason written down in words,
Sedition, sometimes Libel.

He rescued me from burning,
Stored by Mr Bell,
Put to use by this wee man,
At least he kept me well.

And now I travel 'cross the sea,
Satire in words to spread,
Fergus and L'oignon
I will work for them instead!

He knows my inner workings,
We fit like hand and glove,
I am his other woman,
His Bonnie other love!

**

Time and motion

Will we ever understand,
The reason for a fate?
The underlying purpose
Which makes an action great!

What you call disaster,
Was it meant that way?
Or does it bring significance,
To another day?

For we will never see the end,
The final scene and act.
The train of Time keeps rolling on,
Despite our small impact.

A day that's changed, a thing not done
It sounds like one big riddle,
Things of the past affect us now,
But we are in the middle.

The things we do will make a mark.
Somewhere in time to come,
But we may never see that time,
Death may leave us numb.

Writers of our history
See what was left behind,
The do not know the reasons why,
The truth they never find.

The hero and the villain,
The drunkard and the fool,
Songs are writ about their lives,
With music as a tool.

The dead are long since buried,
They lie beneath their stones,
If they could have seen the future,
They may have made old bones.

Is there some higher power?
Dictating how we climb?
Are we only puppets?
On the map of time?

I spilled my all to Roger,
To make him understand,
The consequence of changing things,
Interfering with fates hand,

For travellers can affect things,
By what they leave behind,
And time runs on continually,
To the end of all mankind.

**

Debt of Honour

No prisoners! Was, the order,
No exceptions to the rule,
The thankless task of shooting men,
Who fought to crown, a fool!

Each man was a traitor,
None denied the crime,
Exhausted, starving, wounded,
From that tragic pantomime.

They gave their names, they met their fate,
Brave men to the last.
Wounded men would be shot too,
Their die was also cast.

Who is next? - A voice replied,
Clearly from the gloom,
'Fraser, James,' he, started,
My gaze shot down the room.

Lying in a corner,
sweating, grey and weak,
Long red hair greased down with sweat,
With hardly strength to speak.

There lay Red Jamie Fraser,
Wounded, close to death.
Begging me to shoot him,
Desperation, his last breath.

My brother swore to spare his life,
I cannot let him down.
I'm honour bound to spare this man,
Most wanted by the Crown.

I packed him in a haycart,
Not thinking he'd survive,
Then he turns up at Helwater,
Very much alive.

**

And one more thing!

One more thing...
I beg another favour,
Before I take my leave,
You, and my mother...
And how I was conceived.

I want to know...
No decent man would tell ye,
Some things are not for sharing,
Would ye tell me your first time?
But that's not why yer caring.

I need to know....
No! I did not love her.
No, it was not rape,
No, she was not married,
I'd not a cuckold make!

Did she...?
She did'na ken the meaning,
By all the Saints above,
A headstrong girl, half my age,
She thought herself in love,

Was she....?
Did they mention she was brave?
Those who knew her well,
Courageous in her reckless way,
I heard my father tell.

Were you....?
I will do penance for her death,
until the day I die,
Twas my fault, I am to blame?
A gleam came to his eye,

Then....?
His big hard hand raised to my cheek,
He looked me in the eye,
How could I be sorry,
I am not. So let it lie.

Gone....
Turned on his heel, emotion hid.
He left! his talking done.
Regretful of his actions,
But not sorry he'd a son.

Death's door

I bid them take me up to bed,
I'd lain downstairs too long,
Fever raged around my veins.
I did nae feel too strong.

I stank like death, was hot and cold,
My head it swam and ached,
I could nae fight much longer,
Despite the jokes I made.

I feel my skin is tighter,
I feel my heart beat slow,
I feel the pull of Gods own voice,
Am I ready to let go?

Come Sassenach, please hold me,
Wrap your arms around,
Warm me, make me feel alive,
Your touch will keep me sound.

I saw a tunnel filled with light,
Like an open door,
Voices calling me to come,
Only if, I'm sure.

I felt your hands upon me,
Warm and full of life,
The choice was there, I made it.
Death or you – my wife.

You Bastard, did you die on me!
I felt your heartbeat fade,
You were so cold, I thought you lost.
Was your decision made?

I could have gone so easily,
Twas harder still to stay,
But I know ye need me Sassenach,
Like I need you each day.

**

Kissing the wilderness

The smell of town had left us,
The smell of marsh had gone,
The smell of death and pirates,
The salt smell lingered on,

We climbed up higher,
Through the trees, Seeking fresher air,
The scent of home, the scent of life,
We knew we would find there.

Evolving with surroundings,
Taking on their hue,
I smell the plants the growing life,
The smell of morning dew.

If happiness could be a smell,
A smell I would have last,
It is the smell of wilderness,
Of freshness and of grass,

The smell of musk, the smell of male,
Of green things that he ate,
The smell of fresh killed rabbits,
Slung around his waist.

Stop yer gasping Sassenach,
Yer likely to pass out,
Ye've filled yon bag with greenery,
What are ye about.

He kissed me then, he tasted,
Of all those things and more,
Like kissing all the wilderness,
For all my needs a cure.

He kissed me long, He kissed my hard,
A cough disturbs my dreams,
Round the corner, welcoming,
Here comes Mr Wemyss!

✳✳

Aldwych Farce.

All hell is loose at River Run,
The Lieutenant came by stealth,
His hobbled horse found in a field,
To steal Jocasta's wealth.

We rode at speed from Wilmington,
Horses blown and sweated,
Filthy from the dusty road,
To find what we suspected.

Duncan Innes injured,
Lieutenant Wolff stone dead,
Ulysses gone missing,
A price upon his head.

For Ulysses, had cut Wolff's throat,
Straight from ear to ear.
If they catch him, he will swing,
On this the law is clear.

Where better for a body,
Than to hide it in a tomb,
But in with Hector Cameron,
There isn't any room.

Jamie opened up the crypt,
To find the space was taken,
The corpse of Daniel Rawlings,
If Jocasta's not mistaken.

We'll put him in yer coffin Aunt,
If I may be so bold.
But when he takes the lid off,
The coffin's packed with gold.

we will take Dr Rawlings,
To be buried on our ground
Lieutenant Wolff can take his place,
Sealed in safe and sound,

Seems we had arrived there,
In the nick of time,
Like something from an Aldwych Farce,
Clearing up the crime!

The yarn Jocasta spun us,
Was all a pack of lies!
You'll not part Hector from the gold,
Not even when he dies!

＊＊

Always Forever

I would return, decision made,
I would take that chance,
The years that show upon my face,
Reflecting times advance.

The years have made their mark on me,
A wrinkle here and there,
No longer in the flush of youth,
There's grey now in my hair,

But time goes on, on either side,
He will have aged, a bit,
Has he matured like a fine wine,
Is he still as fit!

I walked into that printer's shop,
My heart was in my mouth,
That warrior frame was still the same,
Nothing had gone south,

I heard the doorbell ringing,
Absorbed still in my work,
Shouted out to Geordie,
His tasks he should not shirk,

But standing there above me,
I thought I'd seen a ghost,
A living Claire, in flesh and bone,
I can touch her, that means most.

And yes! the years have aged me too,
A few more scars she'll find,
Most of them upon my skin,
Several in my mind.

For twenty years I've burned inside,
Thinking she was lost,
I will not let her go again,
No matter what it costs,

This thing that runs between us,
Has never been as strong,
Forever always in my heart,
Those years were not that long.

More beautiful with passing time,
More passionate with age,
Will ye come to bed wi' me?
And start another page.

**

Unrest – Tar and feather bed

Unrest settled on the air,
It hung upon the mist,
Pervasive as the fever
Persuasive as a fist

Change was starting to appear,
Collecting heavy dues
Driving good folk from their homes,
Punished for their views,

The smell of tar was cloying,
The mob was out for blood,
Fuelled by tavern gossip,
They gathered in the mud,

The printer was in hiding,
The shop they sought to burn,
Jamie stood there, broom in hand,
And fought each one in turn.

He swung it in a fiery arc,
Warrior's eyes were gleaming,
Tar was sticking in his hair,
Sweat down his face was streaming,

Joking with the hecklers,
Grandstanding the mob,
Daubing everyone with tar
He saw it as his job.

The crowd was growing restless,
They'd take him with a rush,
Then my Scottish hero
would get tarred with the same brush.

**

The Fiddler on the Roof

They day had been a long one,
He'd just come up to bed,
I was Listening to the house creak,
Thinking what he'd said,

Warm as toast beside him,
My Scottish central heating,
Lay discussing baby names,
Outside It was sleeting.

A voice came from the chimney breast,
Disjointed in the night,
James! it called repeatedly,
I nearly died of fright!

Jamie sitting up in bed,
Hair standing on end,
Cursing like a Scotsman can,
Recognised a friend,

Paris is a dangerous place,
As if I needed proof,
Not a burglar but a Prince,
Is climbing on our roof!

He climbed in through our window,
Clothes in disarray,
Trousers hanging open,
Stockings gone astray,

Informal introductions,
Made in courtly style,
How does one curtsy, when in bed?
The thought raises a smile!

Bitten by her monkey,
He'd tried to leave her room,
But then he found her husband
Was sitting in the gloom.

And that is how I met him,
Our Prince across the sea,
A dishevelled late-night visitor,
Whose fate we'd yet to see.

Jamie gave him brandy,
And gave his hair a comb,
Saddled him our swiftest horse,
For his journey home

Running from a bedroom,
His mistress a bit skittish,
Is like hiding in the heather,
And running from the British!

Seeing Red

Time to make an entrance,
No more to be said,
I glided down the staircase,
In my dress of red!

Murtagh's eyebrows lifted,
He hid a wicked smile,
Coughed and left him to it,
That man just has no guile.

His face went every shade of red,
I did not need to guess,
His thoughts were written on a face,
Redder than the dress,

You want us to be visible,
Yes – but have a care,
I can see down tae yer navel,
Yer pretty neatly bare!

Can ye not just cover up,
A hanky or a shawl,
These Frenchmen don't have my restraint,
And they can see it all!

To make an entrance in the Court,
I know is in the plan,
For Christ's sake Claire be careful,
Take a larger fan!

If I find ye in an alcove,
With a Frenchman, then he's dead,
I promise I won't spank ye,
Other thoughts are in my head!

**

Grand Da has Balls.

So, we sat and talked genetics,
Who could travel, who could not,
Who could neatly roll their tongue,
Depends what gene you got.

The Opal had exploded,
Hot in Jem's small hand,
But cold to Ian and Jamie,
Not glowing like a brand.

Ovaries and Testes,
The roll of eggs and sperm,
The boys are looking sheepish,
In fact, they start to squirm.

Talking of such matters,
Is making Jamie blush,
I never thought him prudish,
But he's having quite a flush.

Out of the mouths of children,
What's testes came the cry,
'Yer balls' replied, his father,
And Grand Da thought he'd die.

Maybe Grand Da 'll show ye,
He's the one wearing a kilt,
Ian got four pen 'orth in,
Blood was nearly spilt.

And so, the boys all left the room,
In the middle Jem's small figure,
Tell me Grand Da – you got balls?
'Aye – but yer Da's are bigger'!

**

Calls in the Forest.

Sat around the fire,
The pipe had gone around,
Stories told of battles,
Some fought on far off ground.

Beer and food and mellow smoke,
And talk of homeland lost,
I began to talk about that time,
The killing and the cost.

Fourteen men, I counted,
I could not call one to mind,
What sort of memory is this?
That makes such killing blind.

Back upon that rain-soaked moor,
My face with tears is sodden,
The earthy smell of peat and gorse,
Weeping for Culloden.

When all but Bird had gone to bed,
I told him of my fears.
That my women saw the future
The awful trail of tears.

Now Bird has sent his mother,
To warm me in my bed,
This is no sense of humour,
She has come to clear my head.

Talk to me Bear Killer,
I will comb your hair,
I hear your words in any tongue,
Your mind I will repair,

The words came out in Gaelic,
To her I bared my soul,
The spectres Grief and Loss and Fear,
The things that kept me whole,

I felt my spirit rising,
And floating up above,
My voice came from a distance,
Softer than a dove.

They will no longer haunt you,
No evil in my heart,
Not here, not now, in this place peace,
At least that is a start.

She combed the tangles from my mind,
Healing words she spoke,
All thoughts of vengeance on that time,
Dispersing with the smoke.

Telephone for Grand Da

Basic Anaesthetics,
Basic equipment too,
Operate on Mandy!
Something I cannot do!

She needs the care of experts,
She needs a special op,
Complex surgery on her heart,
To make the murmur stop.

As soon as they are able,
I know that they must go,
Back through the screaming dark abyss
And we will miss them so.

And so they went, we said goodbye,
Prayed they made it safe,
Back to modern medicine,
To save Young Mandy's life.

I woke alone from restless sleep,
He was outside in the air,
he said had been dreaming,
And they all were safely there.

He'd seen a town like Inverness,
Described to me the Manse,
A study with long windows,
A kind wee brown- haired lass,

An object on a table,
With a club shaped like a bone,
And a tail just like a curly pig.
Is that a Telephone?

Jemmy lifting up the club,
Calling from afar,
Long distance and 200 years,
Phone call for Grand Da!

**

L.O.V.E

Leaving you was hard my dear,
Our ways destined to part,
Vanishing through time and stone,
Escaping, broke my heart.

Let me lay my head down,
On your careworn breast,
Visceral my feelings
Emotion cannot rest.

Lie with me my Sassenach,
Open up you heart,
Venture back into my world,
Embrace what cannot part.

Love me as I love you,
Only that will do,
Vanquish all your final doubts,
Enmeshed for life we two!

**

Outlander Animals

Things you win at dice!

I was in a bar in Wilmington,
Tied up to a wall,
My owner was playing dice,
And losing – I recall.

I had my head down on my paws,
But I wasn't asleep,
My ear was cocked and listening,
In case I had to leap.

I'd never had an owner,
Keep me more than a few days,
I'm half a dog and half a wolf,
With antisocial ways.

Oh, here comes my new one!
He's nothing but a lad,
He seems to be quite proud of me,
Things can't be all that bad

He's going to call me Rollo,
Rollo of the dice.
I've never had a name before
I think that's really nice.

Oooh, he has a family,
This is what I need,
They know I can catch my own fish,
I'm really cheap to feed.

Now I am a, Fraser.
The Frasers are my pack!
Ian is my master,
I'm never looking back.

**

Wolf Brothers

Seeking out adventure,
Was Like falling off a log,
For teenage Ian Murray,
And me, his faithful dog,

Lying at his bedside,
One last watch I'll keep,
Tired, worn out dreaming,
My life replays in sleep.

Wolfs Brother as a Mohawk
I've been right there by his side,
The day he laid down his old life,
And took a Mohawk Bride.

Coming home, I walked with him,
A long and sorrowed trail,
Kept him warm through lonely nights,
My loyalty won't fail.

Indian Scout – I was his right,
Protecting, by his side.
When he is lost, I'm always there,
His best friend and his guide.

I've seen the boy become a man,
We've travelled many miles,
I've protected all his family,
I've seen the children smile.

He's married now and happy,
Friend Rachel keeps his heart,
I am old and stiff with wounds,
But from him I'll not part,

My life was an adventure,
My dreams now melt like the ice,
a good life, for a half wolf dog,
A Scots boy won at dice.

I have no strength to raise my head,
I cannot thump my tail,
My time has come to join the wolves,
On the never-ending trail.

Goodbye my boy, you are a man,
Your life should make you proud,
I am still sitting on your right,
Silent in the crowd.

**

Bacon on the run.

I was born, I know not where!
To market I was taken,
Sold to the highest bidder,
Destined to be bacon.

I love my food, hate my pen.
Those humans are mistaken,
If they think I'll hang around,
And let them make me bacon.

I'm living in the pantry,
Surrounded by their food,
If I decide to eat it all,
That would be seen as rude.

Piglets come and piglets go,
I give them all the talk,
Tell them they should run away,
Before they become pork.

I've found a warm and cosy den,
Down in the foundation
No one dare come near me,
I've bred bacon for the nation.

I've a very simple attitude
When it comes to men,
Eat them or get eaten.
My meat is not for them.

**

'Beware of the Pig!!

In the quest for plumbing,
Roger dug the hole,
A kiln and lots of pipe work,
Was Brianna's goal.

I stood with Roger at its edge,
Chatting, digging done
When good Major Macdonald,
Entered in the fun.

He hadn't seen her coming,
Creeping from her den
Prowling round the corner,
She puts terror into men!

Pig! Shouted Roger –
as best his voice could do,
Pig! I shouted louder,
The Major heard me too.

He broke into a gallop,
Running from the sow,
She grunted and she snuffled,
And followed him, and how.

Running at the double,
This is no time to talk,
The Major trying to escape,
Five hundred pounds of pork.

Pit! We screamed together,
The Major turned his head,
Spurs entangled in his boots,
He fell down just like lead.

The sow was gaining on him,
Back up, he sprints away,
Heading for the kiln pit,
There's not much we could say.

We saw him as he disappeared,
Straight over the edge,
Curled up like a hedgehog,
Protecting meat and veg!

Are ye damaged Major?
His wig was still in place,
Expecting to be eaten,
Said the look upon his face!

Din nae worry Major,
She's given up on that,
Climb out of there in safety,
She's chewing on yer hat!

A verra noisy mule

I miss my days at River Run,
Life was quiet there,
I was a favourite of the mistress,
A mule without a care.

As loud a mule as you will find,
With a voice to raise the dead,
A loyal and a kindly mule,
As long I get fed!

She gave me to her nephew,
That fiery red-haired Scot,
He loads me up with boxes,
He makes me work a lot.

They took me through the forest,
There was thunder and then lightening,
I took off and ran away,
That storm was really frightening.

I am a sort off homing mule,
I came back in the morning,
My bray was heard for miles around,
As the day was dawning.

I've was stolen by the teamsters,
I bit one in the arm,
That very rough man bit me back,
He really had no charm.

I should have been a Fraser,
I'm as stubborn as the boss,
I like to stand right on his foot,
That makes him really cross.

Now I live with Fergus,
As I'm getting rather old.
We have an understanding,
And I never will be sold.

**

Adso – a cat with attitude

I've been captured by a human,
A large human at that,
A big, tall one with ginger hair,
And a very funny hat,

I was lying out, up on the ridge,
Scratching by my ear.
The human stuffed me down his coat,
It's nice and warm in here.

The journey on the horse was wild,
The horse was misbehaving,
So, I crawled into his bag,
A bag that was worth saving.

I think he thought he'd dropped me,
Went back and had a look,
But I was safe inside by then,
Curled up in a nook.

I'd better introduce myself,
I climbed onto their bed,
Then he called me Adso.
'What's one of those? 'I said.

I now work in the surgery,
Catching mice and rats
Everybody has a job,
Even kidnapped cats,

**

Major MacDonald's Wig

Us cats are fussy in our friends,
Independent in our ways,
We come and go just as we like,
It's how we spend our days.

We love to play, we love to hunt,
We can combine the two,
if we can have a bit of fun
That is just what we'll do.

The Major has a curious thing,
It lives upon his head,
It moves sometimes like it's alive,
I'd best make sure it's dead.

I'll stalk it, and I'll pounce on it.
It's really not that big,
Then I'll claw the life from it,
That thing he calls his wig.

I'll wait until he's gone to bed,
And the wig is fast asleep,
Then I'll kill it like a mouse,
Before it makes a squeak.

Get out of here you F'ng cat,
The wig is out of sight,
He picks an item off the floor,
And throws with all his might.

As I dodge the flying boot,
That drives me from his room,
I hear my mistress laughing,
And a door creaks in the gloom.

Safe in the master's bedroom,
I do what nature calls,
forget about MacDonald's wig,
I'd rather lick my balls.

❋❋

Donas – sire of generations

Sorrel coated stallion
A challenge from the start,
Teeth and temper raging,
Would breaking, break your heart,

Auld Alec took ye slowly,
Bid me, take my time.
He did nae want tae ruin ye,
That would be a crime,

Ye did nae like the saddle,
A day I well recall,
Ye took off like a raving loon,
Ye jumped over the wall.

Ye threw me in the brambles,
Dumped me then and there,
Ankle sprained, I had to go,
And get it fixed by Claire.

I'd not admit ye threw me,
And how my seat was lost,
I told old Alec cheerily.
Ye were stung by a wasp.

The bravest, fastest horse I've sat,
The apple of my eye,
There's nought save me can ride ye,
Though young Hamish just might try.

Strong enough to carry two,
Where the ground is level.
Ye'll serve me well ye horse of hell,
Named Donas, for the devil!

**

Gideon

Sour is a perfect word,
To describe this horse,
A mean streak running through him,
He won't be tamed with force.

Bought cheaply for this reason,
A temper that's a try on,
Sound of wind, he'll go all day,
But his mouth is hard as Iron.

He bucks and runs away with you,
He cat-leaps, and he rears!
So quick he'll dump you on your arse,
Or out over his ears.

Only one man rides him,
He's a bastard of a horse,
Impatient and delinquent,
The bosses mount – of course.

Threatened with castration,
But no one ever dares,
He makes the Ridge a fortune,
Serving Indian mares

Mighty man of valour,
The meaning of his name,
It takes one of those to ride him,
James Fraser knows his game!

**

Acknowledgements

As always full acknowledgement is given to the fact that the characters used in these poems are created by Diana Gabaldon and are from the Outlander series of books and the TV Series.

My work is a tribute to her brilliance and the popularity of her novels.

Thanks are given to the users of the social media fan pages where these poems are also published, from these pages I have received constructive criticism, advice on spelling, grammar, and content. Some of you have now also become friends outside of cyber space!

Full credit is also given to a very talented artist who has agreed that I can use her work for the front cover of this book.

Credit to Lynn Fuller for allowing her use of her pastel drawing in this manner.

Other books by the Author

This book is the sixth book in a series of Unofficial Books of Outlander inspired poetry.

Unofficial Droughtlander Relief.

The Droughtlanders Progress.

Totally Obsessed.

Fireside Stories.

Je Suis Prest.

I hope the Princess will Approve – a book of COVID and Horse related poems.

■■■

Ginger like Biscuits - the adventures of a Welsh Mountain Pony.

Copyright

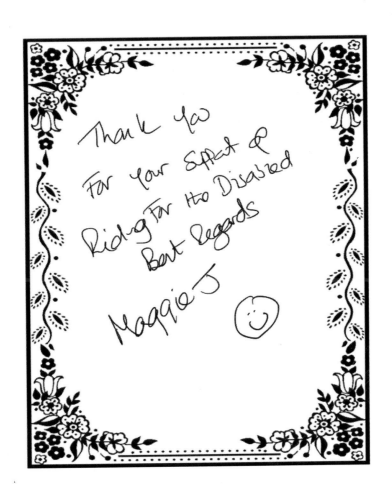

Thank you
For Your Support &
Riding For the Disabled
Best Regards

Maggie J

RDA It's what you can
do that counts

iding for the Disabled Association
corporating Carriage Driving